Ti and Tiger

OTHER TITLES IN THE SAME SERIES

Gita and Goldie
0 7475 3879 4 (hbk)
0 7475 3656 5 (pbk)

Gita and her sister Manveer love their pet dog
Goldie. Then Gita and Manveer have an argument,
and Gita decides to run away. Will Goldie be able to
help find her?

Becky and Beauty
0 7475 3880 8 (hbk)
0 7475 3566 3 (pbk)

Becky has decided that she is going to sell her pony
Beauty. Beauty is no good in competitions, and Becky
wants to win! But one stormy day something happens that
makes Becky think again . . .

Paul and Percy
0 7475 3881 6 (hbk)
0 7475 3567 1 (pbk)

Paul loves going to visit Mrs Sage – and Percy, her
parrot. Then Mrs Sage falls ill, so Percy comes to live
with Paul. But Percy refuses to speak any more – until
one incredible day!

Timmy and Tiger

MARY HOOPER

Illustrated by
Lucy Su

BLOOMSBURY
CHILDREN'S
BOOKS

First published in Great Britain in 1998
Bloomsbury Publishing Plc, 38 Soho Square, London, W1V 5DF

Copyright © Text Mary Hooper 1998
Copyright © Illustrations Lucy Su 1998

·   The moral right of the author has been asserted
A CIP catalogue record of this book is available from the
British Library

ISBN 0 7475 3878 6 (hbk)
ISBN 0 7475 3564 7 (pbk)

Printed in England by Clays Ltd, St Ives plc

10 9 8 7 6 5 4 3 2

Cover design by Mandy Sherliker

Contents

Contents

Chapter One

Luke kicked the ball and it shot past Timmy. It rolled under one of the bushes against the fence.

'Goal!' Luke shouted, leaping up and down.

'Okay,' Timmy said. 'You win.' And he pushed his way into the bush to find the ball.

'I'm soaked. I'm going home!' Timmy heard Luke

calling. It had been sunny when they'd come out, but now it was pouring with rain. 'See you tomorrow?'

Timmy didn't reply. He'd heard something moving around in one of the bushes.

'What's up?' Luke called. 'Can't you find the ball?'

'There's something in here,'
Timmy said. He dropped on all
fours so he could see properly.
'A wild animal.'

'Oh yeah?' Luke said. 'What
is it – a wild boar?'

'Maybe . . .' Timmy said.

'I'm getting soaked!' Luke
called. 'I'm off home.'

Timmy saw a sudden

movement under the bush.
'Hey!' he said softly. 'Hello, boy!'

A pair of eyes looked back at him. A pair of green, frightened eyes in a face of damp, ginger fur.

'Here, puss, puss!' Timmy breathed. The cat backed further into the bush.

'It's okay. I won't hurt you!' Timmy said. 'Come on, you can come home with me. I'll give you something to eat. Food!'

The cat opened its mouth in a silent miaow.

'There. You understood that, didn't you?' Timmy put his hand out. 'Here, puss. You can

10

have a nice saucer of milk. And some of Wolf's dog food, eh?'

In the dim light under the bush, the cat's eyes seemed to glow.

'Wolf is Pete's dog,' Timmy said softly. 'He's a big ugly

thing. But okay, really.
Nothing to be scared of.'

All the time he was talking
he was moving his hand closer
to the cat. 'You're lost, aren't
you, boy?' he said. His fingers
touched fur and stroked it.

'You come home with me and I'll look after you.'

As he spoke, Timmy reached for the cat. Grasping it gently, he moved backwards on all fours until he was out of the bush.

He stood up, holding the cold, shivering cat tightly in his

arms. 'You're soaking!' he said.
He rolled up the cat in the
bottom half of his sweatshirt.
'I'm going to take you home
with me and look after you!'
He stroked the cat gently. 'And

although you don't look much like one – I'm going to call you Tiger.'

Chapter Two

'I'll sort you out,' Timmy whispered to Tiger. 'I'll give you some food and make you warm. And I might be allowed to keep you.' As he said that he crossed his fingers, knowing very well that he *wouldn't* be allowed to keep Tiger.

Timmy loved animals but he'd taken home too many

stray things in the past. Once
there had been a hamster that
had bitten his mum's finger.
After that there had
been a mouse that
had got loose in the
kitchen. And then there had
been a rabbit which had eaten
half the flowers in the garden.
So it wasn't very likely that

Timmy's mum was going to let him keep Tiger . . .

As they went through the back door of Timmy's house, Tiger was still lying hidden in the fold of his big sweatshirt.

'Now, just lie still,' Timmy whispered. 'Don't move!' With a bit of luck, he thought, his

mum wouldn't notice anything odd.

'Timmy! Look at the state of you!'

Timmy stood in the doorway, ball under his arm, bulge in his jumper.

'Take those boots off!' his mum ordered. 'Chuck that ball outside. Then go upstairs and get in the bath.'

Wolf got up from his basket in front of the radiator and padded up to Timmy. He could sniff the smell of cat.

'Shoo!' Timmy said, trying to get his boots off without squashing Tiger.

'I could see you from the window,' Mum said. 'I thought

to myself – why on earth are
those boys playing in the
pouring rain? And then I saw
you coming across the road
muttering to yourself!'

'I was . . . er . . . working out
a sum in my head,' Timmy
fibbed.

He began to make his way
across the kitchen. He held on
to Tiger with one hand, and
pushed Wolf away with the
other. He'd nearly made it
when . . .

'Why have you got your
jumper rolled up like that?'
Mum suddenly asked.

'Because it's muddy,' Timmy said. 'I'll take it off and rinse it.'

'What?!' His mum said in surprise. 'Since when have you ever . . .'

But Timmy didn't hear the rest, because he was leaping up the stairs two at a time.

Safe in his room, he carefully unrolled his sweatshirt and put the wet, shivering Tiger down on the floor. He looked scared.

'And skinny!' Timmy said. 'Bet you haven't had a decent meal for weeks. Hope you like dog food.'

Turning his sweatshirt inside out, he dried Tiger, then put him on the bed and covered

him with part of the duvet.

'Stay here,' he said. 'I'm going to look for food.'

Tiger gave a short mioaw, then yawned and put his head down on his paws.

'Mission – Moggy!' Timmy said to himself, and he put on his dressing gown and went downstairs.

Chapter Three

'Aren't you in that bath yet?'
Mum asked when he went in
the kitchen.

'In a minute,' Timmy said.
'I'm a bit hungry.'

'Supper in an
hour,' Mum said,
and added, 'and
don't spoil your
appetite!'

'Just a biscuit,' Timmy said.
He opened the fridge, hoping to
see an opened tin of dog food.

'The biscuits aren't in the
fridge,' his mum said.

And nor was the dog food.
Timmy closed the fridge. He
wished that his mum would go
into another room.

'I'll have some milk, then,' he
said. He opened the fridge
again.

'You don't drink milk!'

'I do today,' Timmy said. 'I
just feel like it.' He poured some
milk from the carton into a
mug. He really wanted to pour
some into a saucer. He thought

his mum might get a bit suspicious about that, though.

'Feeling all right, are you?' Mum said. 'First you tell me you're rinsing your sweater, next you're drinking milk. In a minute you'll be telling me you want to help me cook supper.'

Timmy looked at the worktop. 'What are we having?'

'Sausages and mash.'

Sausages! Timmy was sure that cats liked sausages.

'Yep, I'll help!' he said. 'What do I have to do?'

'Don't be silly,' Mum said. 'Just go and get in that bath!'

Timmy suddenly pointed out of the window. 'What's that?!' he asked. When his mum

looked, he made a grab for a
raw sausage.

Mum smacked his wrist.
'What are you playing at? Get
up those stairs. I don't want to
see you again until you're
clean!'

Timmy went upstairs and
started looking about in his

room for something to pour the milk into. 'I'll get you some food as soon as I can,' he said to Tiger. 'Maybe some of Wolf's food when he gets fed. Or a sausage. Do you like sausages? I might even go out to buy you a proper tin of cat food or . . .'

Timmy didn't hear the door opening. All he heard was a

short scream, and then Mum saying in a very cross voice, 'What on earth's that scrawny-looking thing doing on your bed?!'

Chapter Four

Timmy explained about Tiger.
He said he was lost, alone,
starving and miserable. But
even before he'd finished, Mum
was shaking her head.

'No, I'm sorry, Timmy. We
can't possibly afford another
pet in the house.' She'd got
Tiger off the bed and now he
was sitting on the floor looking

up at them. 'Especially pets
that look as scruffy as that
one.'

'But he only looks like that
because he's been sleeping
rough!' Timmy said. 'I bet
someone threw him out.'

'I can't say I'm surprised,'

said Mum. 'Not exactly a *pretty* cat, is he?'

'He will be when he's clean and dry,' Timmy said. 'He just wants feeding up a bit and looking after.'

Mum sat down on the bed. 'Besides, I've never been that keen on cats.'

Tiger moved closer to Timmy, rubbing himself against Timmy's foot.

Timmy put down a hand and

stroked him. 'Oh, please let me keep him, Mum!' he said. 'Pete's got Wolf, but I haven't got anyone!'

Mum shook her head. 'I just can't afford it.'

'He'll eat scraps!'

'No, Timmy. He'd have to have proper cat food, and milk – and there would be flu injections and vet's bills. No, you'd better say goodbye to the cat now, before you get too fond of him.'

'I'm fond of him already,' Timmy said. Scruffy and scraggy though he was, Timmy felt there was something special about Tiger. That he wasn't just an ordinary cat.

'Can I just keep him a few weeks to feed him up?'

'No, Timmy.'

'A week, then.'

'No!'

'A day. What difference can a day make?' Timmy pleaded. 'You won't even know he's here!'

'It's best if . . .'

'Oh, Mum!' Timmy's eyes filled with tears.

His mum sighed. 'One night, then. But tomorrow, after school, you take him straight down to the animal rescue place. And I don't want to hear another word about it!'

Timmy sniffed back tears.

'Not another word! I've said

tomorrow and that's what I mean. And it's to come downstairs tonight and sleep in the kitchen. I don't want it up here with all its fleas.'

Timmy was quite sure Tiger didn't have fleas, but he wasn't going to argue with Mum. 'I'll fix him up with a box in front of the radiator,' he said eagerly, 'and, Mum – can he have a sausage to eat?'

Chapter Five

By supper time Tiger had eaten
two sausages, a saucer of
Wolf's tinned dog food and a
plate of cornflakes with lots of
milk.

When Pete, Timmy's brother,
came in, Tiger was sitting near
Wolf's basket in the kitchen,
cleaning his paws and looking
quite at home.

Pete stood in the kitchen
doorway and looked at the cat.
'What's that tatty old thing?'

'That's my cat,' Timmy said
proudly. 'I found him in the
park.'

'That scruffy thing's not a

cat!' Pete jeered. 'It's a scrubbing brush on legs.'

'He's not!' Timmy said hotly. 'He's a *lovely* cat. Aren't you, Tiger?'

'Tiger!' Pete said. 'I've never

seen anything that looks less
like a tiger.'

Timmy pointed at Pete's dog.
'Well, he doesn't look like a
wolf!'

Pete clapped his hands. 'Get
that cat, Wolf! See him off!'

Wolf was stretched out full
length in his basket. He opened
one eye and looked at Tiger.

'Cats!' Pete said. 'Go!'

Tiger looked at Wolf. Wolf
shut his eye again.

'See,' Timmy said. 'My
Tiger's not scared of your
soppy dog! My Tiger's a super-
cat, he's . . .'

'That's enough,' Mum said.
'Go and wash your hands
before you eat. And Timmy,

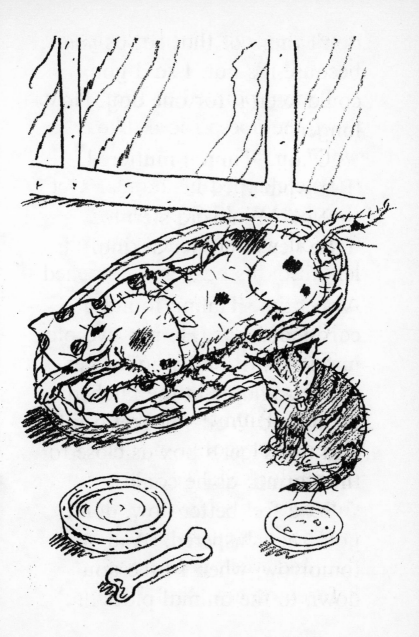

don't think of that cat as *yours*, because it's not. I said you could keep it for one day. No longer.'

'Okay,' Timmy muttered. 'But what if I . . .'

'No!' Mum said sternly. 'Don't even bother asking.'

At bedtime Timmy found a cardboard box. He put two old jumpers in it and stood it next to the radiator in the kitchen. He moved Wolf's basket a little and got Tiger's box as close to the warmth as he could.

'You feel better now, don't you?' he whispered. 'And tomorrow, when I take you down to the animal place . . .'

For a moment Timmy felt all
choked up. 'Mum – what do
they do with cats at the animal
rescue place?' he asked.

'They feed 'em to dogs!' Pete
said. He moved the cat's box
away from the radiator. He
moved Wolf's basket closer.

'Don't be silly,' Mum said.

'No, Timmy, they find them good homes. Homes with people who can afford to keep them.'

'But what if . . .'

'Bed!' Mum said, pointing.

Timmy gave Tiger one last hug. Pete had gone out of the room, so Timmy moved the

cat's box back in front of the radiator. 'Night-night,' he said to him. 'Sleep tight. See you in the morning.'

Chapter Six

Timmy stayed awake for ages, trying to think of ways to earn cash so he could keep Tiger. If only he hadn't spent all his birthday money on toy cars . . .

He didn't want to think of Tiger down at the animal rescue place, lost and alone. Timmy already felt that Tiger

was his. He was *meant* to belong to him.

Timmy worried and fretted, but at last, still unable to think of a way out, he fell asleep.

The clock in the hall downstairs had just chimed three when he suddenly woke again. For a moment he just lay there, and then he realised that there was something tickling his face. Something warm and wet and a bit rough. Tiger's tongue!

'What are *you* doing here?' Timmy murmured. 'Mum will kill you if she knows . . .'

Tiger licked Timmy's face all over.

'What are you doing, you

daft cat,' Timmy giggled
sleepily. 'It's not morning yet
. . .' His eyes closed again. He
was about to drift back to sleep
when Tiger started miaowing
loudly.

Miaow . . . miaow . . . miaow,
Tiger went, quickly and
urgently.

'What's the matter?' Timmy murmured. 'What do you want?'

Tiger miaowed on, so Timmy sat up and put on the light.

And then he smelled it.

Smoke!

Timmy gasped, ran to the door and looked down into the hall. Smoke was coming from

under the sitting-room door,
curling up the stairs in grey,
wispy spirals. Listening, he
could hear a noise from the
sitting-room: a frightening,
crackling, burning noise.

Timmy scooped up Tiger.
'Fire!' he yelled at the top of his
voice. 'Mum! Pete!' He ran to

their doors and flung them
open. 'Fire! Get out quickly!'

• • •

'So this is the hero, is it?' said
the fireman, clapping Timmy
on the shoulder.

It was two hours later.
Everyone – including Wolf –
was safe. The fire was out and

Timmy, Pete and Mum were sitting in their pyjamas having a cup of tea.

'Yes, it was Timmy who woke us all up,' Mum said proudly.

Timmy shook his head. 'No, it wasn't me,' he said, 'it was Tiger. My cat.'

'What?!' said Mum.

'No!' said Pete.

'Is that right?' said the fireman.

'He woke me up. He came on the bed and licked my face, and then he miaowed loudly. It's *him* who's the hero . . .' Timmy picked up Tiger. 'I will be able to keep him now, won't I, Mum?'

Mum smiled, sighed, sipped
her tea. 'Of course you can,' she
said. 'We'll manage somehow.'

'I'll buy him a basket,' Pete
said. 'It can be next to Wolf's
basket in the kitchen.'

'I'll get his photo in the local paper!' the fireman said. 'Brave cat saves family!'

'Hear that?' Timmy said to Tiger. 'You're going to be a star!'

OTHER YOUNG FICTION SERIES

THE TIGERS:
Ghost Goalie 0 7475 3925 1 (hbk) /3846 8 (pbk)
Save the Pitch 0 7475 3926 X (hbk) /3847 6 (pbk)
The Terrible Trainer 0 7475 3927 8 (hbk) /3850 6 (pbk)
The Cup Final 0 7475 3928 6 (hbk) /3851 4 (pbk)

**"We're the Tigers . . . Hear us roar.
Seven-nil will be the score!"**

The Tigers are the best under-ten football team around – and they know it. The preamble is always unpredictable, but they have fun facing each new challenge with unbridled enthusiasm and always win in the end – even if it is a close run thing!

CRAZY GANG:
"Og Fo" says the Space Bug 0 7475 3929 4 (hbk) /3562 0 (pbk)
"Do I Look Funny to You?" 0 7475 3930 8 (hbk) /3561 2 (pbk)
Pets Just Want to Have Fun 0 7475 3931 6 (hbk) /3560 4 (pbk)
"I Don't Like Space Glop" 0 7475 3932 4 (hbk) /3563 9 (pbk)

Enjoy the zany, mad-cap world of Max and Pat, and their space friends Jazz and Zug Zug, in these fun-filled books. When Pat the dog and Zug Zug the space bug meet, they just want to have fun – but they can't help causing trouble! Join Max and Jazz trying to keep an eye on their pets, and having a crazy time along the way!